THE WORD SPIDER

Chris Horn

The Word Spider

Disclaimer

The characters and events of The Word Spider are fictional (as far as I know, there are no secret kingdoms of mini beasts outside an abandoned bookshop)
If you happen to know of any such place, this is coincidental.

Although mankind is responsible for untold damage to the environment, we have not yet reached the levels of destruction described in the Word Spider. If we look after our world, from the smallest arachnids to the biggest creatures on land or in the sea, we will have a home for many years to come.

You can find out more, on how to help bugs and insects here https://www.rspb.org.uk/get-involved, or how to take part in a beach clean https://www.nationaltrust.org.uk/lists/pitch-in-with-a-beach-clean.

There are many more web-pages, with great ideas and suggestions on how we can all help look after our planet.

To my children, be brave like Alice and follow your dreams. There's a whole world out there to explore.

On the edge of town in an abandoned bookshop, under the floorboards in the dark dusty space filled with decades worth of forgotten things (buttons, coins, a discarded photo showing a family surrounded by books from the distant past), there is a whole world in constant caliginosity.

Veiled in a midnight darkness stands a tiny hamlet of houses made from bits and bobs left many years ago by mankind. A bottle, a shoe, old boxes; an oddity of things long discarded by man. The bigger dwellings were made from stone and wood. The residents of this hodgepodge of houses were unique in their appearance, covered head to toe in fur as white as snow.

In charge of the little, hidden community was a kind, handsome spider, covered in soft white fur, muscular but with a little middle-age spread, and father to Alice and George.

Their father's firm, but loving ways ensured they all stayed safe, hidden away in their little world away from most of the other creatures.

Although man had long left the Earth, there were threats. Some creatures did not abide by the law of the land and would do anything for a meal. Here in the village, there was often hunger and bellies that needed filling, but the albinos made do and lived a peaceful, secluded life.

Everyone in the little spider world was content, living this way, scavenging for food, learning the ways of spiders and not making a fuss; everyone, that is, apart from young Alice.

Alice wanted adventure, to travel beyond their home, to see the world, but most of all she wanted to learn to read. She understood the meaning of the written word, the power each one held, and believed they could help all the creatures of the world.

Alice's father, like his before him and as far back as anyone could remember, believed that spiders had no need for reading nor adventure. He felt they should just be happy with what they had.

Standing in the corner of her room, Alice listened as her father went over the same speech he always did when she asked about learning to read.

"What use are words! Can they find food?"

Alice's brother laughed from inside his bedroom door.

"Can they help build a web?"

Laughter again, at the sight of Alice being scorned by their father.

"Tell me one good thing reading will do?"

Alice looked around, trying to think of the words, but her tongue became twisted.

Her brother laughed again. This time she had had enough. For too long now she had listened to the same speech, to the lack of thinking from her father. She loved her family dearly and wanted only the best for them, but she could no longer hold back the tears and anguish, so she fled, out into the little town square and off through the tunnels into the unknown.

The anger and upset burst like a dam, and crying as she ran, Alice's tears fell to the dusty floor.

Her legs took her as far as they could, between floorboards and past rusty nails, splintered, decade-old joists and further still.

Soon she became lost within the dusty gloom, her anger subsiding, her mind imagining things lurking in the surrounding darkness.

What had she done? Her family would never forgive her for this!

With panic setting in, she didn't know what to do. Fear of the shadows around her and fear of returning home caused her to stand motionless for what seemed like an eternity.

Then as her tears dried, and her eyes cleared, up ahead she started to make something out. There, only a short distance away, she could see a slim sliver of light, breaking through a crack in the plaster.

Edging forward, closer and closer, her heart felt as if it would burst. Was this what she had dreamed of; had she found a way to the outside world?

Alice stepped towards the splintered wood, she peered through into the space beyond, and on the other side there lit up by the late afternoon sun, in all its dirt and grime covered glory, was a bookshop and its wondrous word-filled treasures.

Rows upon rows of books covered in dust and dirt sat there for longer than she knew, with no one left to read them or flick through their word filled pages. Their covers had faded with time. Alice could only guess at what stories they contained.

Her mind drifted back to her father and his other favourite saying: "Words lead to knowledge, knowledge to power, and power corrupts everything."

No one knew what had really happened to the humans, and her father used that as another excuse for spiders not to read.

"They had the power of words, they read and told stories, and look what happened to them!"

Alice knew there was more to words than just the corrupted evil that her father portrayed. Words lit up the darkest night and sparked imaginations in young and old, with stories passed down through generations; remembering those who had been before and giving hope for those to come.

Sitting on the edge of the small hole formed in the long-splintered wood, she realised that this was it. If she went through and carried on this journey, she knew she would probably never see her family again. If she went back, she would remain in the family home and the little hamlet for the rest of her life.

She had always wanted adventure, to see the world, to experience the unknown; and more than anything, she wanted to learn to read.

Alice stepped through.

She had never seen so much space, so much light, growing up in the confines of the dust-filled floorboards. She stood in awe, scared yet excited at the surrounding vastness.

Where should she begin this adventure? None of her family had dared to try such things.

She had no stories or tales on which to plan her next move. This was all new, the first to step beyond their little world and out into what lay beyond.

Climbing up the long-faded wallpaper hanging to the wall with only the slightest grip. Deciding that higher would be better, Alice, from her position up above, was able to see the whole world before her. Each step was slow and dangerous, the wallpaper was old and flaky, and more than once she had to stop and change her course. As light as she was, she was still able to cause the paper to pull away from the wall and fall to the floor below.

Finally, after what seemed like hours, she reached the curve of the ceiling and paused for breath. Alice looked back towards where she had come, and was already beyond even her wildest dreams. None of her family would ever believe that she had been this far, which made her realise just how little they were and how big the world was.

It was getting dark, and the setting red orb of the Sun was dropping below the broken windows around her. Soon the store would be in shadow, not as dark as the spiders' home but dark enough for unimaginable creatures to be roaming around.

Alice decided to find somewhere she could spend the night, and followed the curve of the ceiling.

But she was unable to find anywhere that would be safe to be alone, and kept herself moving one step after another. The Sun continued to set, and the room grew darker and darker. Panic started to creep into her head, which was made worse by fear of the unknown and being away from her family for the first time in her life.

She was about to give up and turn for home. Her eyes having grown up in the perpetual darkness of her home started to adjust to the gloom. But this was a different kind of darkness, unfamiliar and foreboding.

With every rustle of paper and the click of a pebble far below, her imagination ran wild, and she started to think of what could be hiding in the shadows. With every sound the monsters multiplied.

Suddenly the room started to brighten, shadows withdrew, and tiny shards of glass on the distant floor sparkled. As the light grew, the shadows withdrew and her fear subsided. What was this magic, where was the light coming from? She moved further around the curve of the ceiling, her excitement growing once more.

Then she saw it. There, through the broken window, was the most magnificent sight; a sky full of millions upon millions of tiny sparks, each twinkling and dancing to its own tune.

Alice could not believe her eyes, having never seen stars before. Her Grandma had told stories of how the sun chased the moon and other fantastic tales of the world outside, but neither she nor her brother truly believed them. Even now seeing with her own eyes, Alice felt disbelief that something so beautiful, so mesmerising, could exist.

The thought of sleep and the ache in her legs had receded to the back of her mind, as she was now feeling a renewed energy with the urge to see more.

She walked along the ceiling towards the broken window, through which the stars shone. The glass had long ago fallen to the ground. Alice could smell the cool autumn breeze, flowing through the now-defunct frame.

No spider alive had been outside the shop, and not many had been beyond the borders of their home. None would have dared to think of such an adventure.

What dangers lurked outside she didn't know. As her mind wandered, she paused, but, adrenaline flowing, she thought to herself that she couldn't stop now.

The wooden frame was cracked, the paint blistered, worn, and cold to the touch. Slowly, she climbed the ridge of the empty frame and into the long-abandoned human world.

In the sky was the most beautiful sight. There was no smog from pollution caused by the old machines of mankind, no artificial light from the now-broken, rusted streetlamps. There in the crystal-clear and star-filled night sky was the moon, floating like some magical orb, huge round and bright, bigger than anything Alice could have ever imagined.

Alice stood and stared for an eternity. The moon shone back at Alice, watching her from afar, neither of them any wiser that in the shadows there was someone or something else watching them.

Settling down in an old, rusted pipe, Alice (who had no idea what its use would have been) felt a sense of safety from its warmth and the moonlight which shone in. She soon fell asleep wishing her family were there to see these amazing sights. She knew if they were there, they would only have argued and convinced her to return to the darkness under the floorboards.

In the shadows the watcher stayed, watching Alice's sleeping form, puzzling over this creature so white and small!

The watcher in the shadows had defended these lands for many moons, and this strange, ghost-white creature wasn't going to destroy the peace. He decided to wait and see what this strange creature was going to do.

Alice woke, hunger in her tummy. She had been hungry before, but the adventures from the previous day had taken its toll, and now she felt exhausted.

She climbed down from the pipe. The sun was rising and the beauty from the night before had been replaced by a deep red light. Alice needed to find food. Slowly and reluctantly, she headed back inside, knowing that within the dust there would be mites, not her favourite food but needs must, and these would keep her going until she could find a more satisfying meal.

The climb down was easier. She spun a thread, and lowered herself to the floor. Her hunger was starting to grow, and she was feeling more unwell than she had in her entire life. She became weak and her mind fuzzy, then off to her side she thought she saw movement, something in the shadows. Alice was not sure if it was her mind playing tricks on her, but she sensed she was being watched.

"Don't be silly. They were just stories to get little spiders to behave," she scolded herself, letting her mind run away with itself.

She kept moving, looking for anything to eat, kicking up dust as she went, but no mites were to be found. She looked around hoping to find anything. Even moss would be welcome right now. Her Gran had shown her and her brother the best things to eat, and Alice paid attention to her Granny since they shared the same taste for adventure and the same desire for more than the spider way of living.

The dust laid thick on the floor, undisturbed for many years, with no sign of anyone having been there before. Alice had trouble walking through the deep layers of dust, like a mountaintop covered in fresh snow; not that she had ever seen snow. They'd lived in the darkness below the floorboards with very little changes in weather, just perpetual dusk; slightly colder in the winter and humid in the summer.

She turned the corner of an old bookshelf, towering meters above her. It was covered in more dust. She looked at the rows of books, unsure what the lettering said, and wished again that she could read. What would these books tell her, what magic hid inside their worn and faded covers!

There in the distance, she smiled to see some mushrooms growing in a dark, shadowy corner just out of reach from the beams of light from the burning red sun. Excited, she scampered over to the patch, fighting through the dust and trying not to choke as each footstep caused an eruption of tiny particles. She was ready to fill her now-empty stomach. The joy of finding this bounty made her forget her surroundings. She grabbed at the closest mushroom, a small button of fungi, that looked as if it could only have just burst through the thin layer of dirt it now nested on. It was fresh-looking and unmarked. Her mouth watered at the thought of the tasty looking morsel. With her attention on the mushroom, Alice was unaware of the creature stalking her, and as she took a mouthful, the beast pounced.

The creature pinned Alice to the floor, jaws snapping and trying to bite her. Alice struggled, striking out with her legs and trying to fight her way free, the way she would when fighting with her brothers. Though she wasn't small for her age, this creature was so much bigger and stronger. Alice wasn't sure how long she would be able to keep fighting it off.

The creature bit one of her legs, and Alice screamed in pain. She cried out as she tried to fight her way free, scratching at its eyes and using all her might. If she was going to die, she would go down fighting.

Rolling with all her weight, she managed to get on top of the creature. She sprayed the last of her web, covering its ghastly mouth with the sticky, silken thread. As the creature clawed at its own face, Alice used the opportunity to run, heading for the books. She thought if she could make it, maybe she could hide from this thing. She looked back to see that the beast had cleared the last threads of webbing from its face and was bounding through the dust. It would soon be upon her, and if it caught her, she knew she was going to die.

Climbing onto the shelf, she looked left and right. There, a short distance away, no more than four or five books of length, she could see a gap to hide in. She ran with all her might, but it was too late, the hunter grabbed her with its tail and pulled her into the dust.

She looked at its face. It had long, pointed whiskers - some broken and ragged. It looked at her. Showing its rows of yellow stained teeth, the creature smiled, and the look said it all: it was going to kill her, and it was going to enjoy it.

Its mouth now was so close to her neck that Alice could feel its rancid breath on her face. She thought about her family and a tear formed at the corner of her eyes. Closing them, she knew this was the end.

But the end never came.

Alice opened her eyes and looked up, seeing a flash of silver...and then she passed out from the exhaustion.

She woke up hungrier and more tired than she had ever been in her life.

How was she even alive?

She felt like she was being carried, and, still dizzy and weak, she passed out again.

There were voices all around her. Alice wasn't sure what they were saying, but they seemed to be arguing. Some words were in base animal, the natural language of the animal kingdom. She'd not seen many other creatures but the odd visiting bug who would stop by trading and use it to communicate with the elders.

She awoke again a time later. The voices had left. There was a fire burning in a small pit to the side, and she could smell food cooking.

"You're awake"

The voice was soft and gentle. She turned over in the cot. There in front of her was a spider, not albino like her and her family, covered in a soft brown fur. She noticed how much bigger he was. Muscular, well-fed, and - she blushed at the thought - quite handsome.

"Who are you, where am I?"

"You're safe, don't worry."

He smiled and gestured at the food cooking in a small pot.

"Are you hungry? You never got to eat your mushroom when the rat attacked you."

"A rat, I never expected them to be so big and -"

"Ugly!" The boy laughed.

"Yes ugly. Was it you who saved me?"

"Me and my spear."

As he said spear, he held out a long stick with the most beautiful tip. She had never seen such a thing. They had no need for weapons in the dark where they hid and waited. They would never dream of attacking anyone or fighting. Who was this boy, and what sort of spiders lived here in the open?

Looking towards the food, she climbed out of bed. Her leg hurt. She ached all over from the fight. Someone had bandaged her wounds and a sticky salve covered them.

The boy offered to help, but she didn't want to look any weaker than she was, so she made her own way to the table.

Waiting whilst Alice had had her fill, the boy sat quietly watching her, as amused by the strange white spider as she was of him.

"I'm Prince Tellon, of Wat-So-e."

"Sorry, of where?"

"Where have you come from? The land of Wat-so-e." As he said this, he gestured at everything around them.

"This is Wat-So-e," he said again. "My father is the king."

"I'm sorry, I have never heard of this place. My family lives far away in the dark. I ran from them, after an argument, and now I'm here and don't know what to do."

"You can start by telling me your name."

She blushed at her lack of manners. She wasn't used to meeting new people, yet the prince had been so kind to her. She stood and curtsied, unsure if that was the right thing to do.

"My name is Alice, just Alice."

The prince laughed.

"There is no need for that, 'Alice, Just Alice'."

She laughed, feeling at ease at his joke.

The prince showed her around the kingdom. She had never seen so many creatures, bugs, spiders, even ones that flew; all working together, drinking and chatting. No one seemed to be hungry or going without.

Children played, laughed, and then she saw them. A whole group sat around in a circle as one of them held a book. They were reading.

"This place is amazing! Why have I never heard of it? My family has lived in the darkness for as long as any of us can remember."

"It may look ideal, but it hasn't always been so. My father's father fought hard to get us here. The rats tried to take it from us so many times, but we have always stood our ground."

They continued to walk the city, trying foods, speaking to other creatures. The prince introducing her as Lady Alice. It was like she was in a dream. Finally, they headed back to the castle to meet the king and queen. Alice was nervous she had never met royalty.

Entering the great hall, Alice was again amazed by it all: statues stood along the walls, soldiers guarded the doors, and in the middle sat the king and queen.

She stopped as Tellon had told her to, curtsied and waited. The wait seemed like an age. The king stared at her; the queen sat like a statue.

"I am King Bracus of Wat-So-E, ruler of this land and protector of all."

The prince stepped forward, looking kindly at Alice.

"This is Lady Alice, of... of..."

He looked at Alice, mouthing *what is your land called?*

"Your Highness my land has no name. I am no lady; I am just a spider"

"Just a spider? Spiders are the leaders of the world! We have been around for millennia and have always been there, in times of need, when Man left this place, after they had poisoned the air so all the large creatures including themselves could no longer walk the earth. We made sure that the creatures that were left worked together."

The queen gently reached for the king's arm, stopping him mid-rant. He looked at Alice and smiled.

"I'm sorry, I just get passionate about our heritage. Where is this land you come from, and how many of you are there?"

Alice explained all: her journey, where she lived and all about her family. The king sat and listened, and the queen smiled as Alice told of how the prince had saved Alice from the rat.

"That may be a problem. We've not dealt with the rats for several years. It's been an uneasy truce. They leave us alone, and we do not go near their lands." As he said this, he looked at his son with a sad look.

"Father, if I may?"

The king nodded at the prince.

"Sir, I had seen Alice the evening before. She came through a crack in the wall and then settled down at the outpost on the roof. I knew she was different and kept watch. When the rat attacked, I couldn't just sit by."

"I know, my son, I have taught you to be more than a bystander and appreciate that you did so with the best intentions in mind. We will just have to keep watch as the rats won't take it lightly."

The queen stood and walked towards them. Should Alice curtsey again? She wasn't sure. The queen looked at Alice, giving a warm smile.

"Come young lady, let's talk while the men figure what to do."

She took Alice's arm and led her away.

"What do you mean they attacked you?"

The Elder Rat was angrier than Corpus had ever seen. After being attacked he had run home, thinking that the Elder would back him and exact revenge. Instead, he had shouted at Corpus, belittling him in front of the others.

"I found a spider outside the city; she wasn't like them. She was white."

"White?"

"Yes, with red eyes. She was small, weak, and had spirit, but I bettered her and was about to finish her when the prince attacked me."

"Interesting. You may have solved a very old mystery."

The elder turned and walked back to his chamber, leaving Corpus alone. He waited a short while before sulking off to plot his own revenge on the prince.

Corpus met with his friends in their normal hangout, an old waste pipe that ran under the rubble-strewn street outside the store. Enjoying a meal, having found some mouldy old corpse of a long dead bird, they talked about adventures most had not lived. They made up brave deeds and heroic encounters. But Corpus knew that none of his friends had even been outside the rat's boundary, let alone had a fight with a snake, and further, let alone a spider.

He jumped onto the back of the closest rat, biting down on the creature's earlobe and taking a chunk out of the smaller rat. The squeal echoed through the drain, and as the two rolled around fighting, the others cheered them on. This was the closest they got to any real adventure but what Corpus was about to suggest would make them all famous.

He sat and explained what had taken place, and how he wanted revenge on the spiders and their kingdom. He had been made to look weak and small, and the Elder had dismissed his claim.

They encouraged each other, egging each other on, coming up with more and more extravagant plans, even saying they would take the kingdom and make it their own to command. By the time they had picked the carcass clean of any flesh, they decided that they would leave that night and capture the albino, and present her as a gift to their leader.

Alice and the prince were touring the kingdom, past fields, hamlets and more. Alice couldn't believe the abundance of food, with all the mushrooms and berries growing freely all around. Children played happily and, in the distance, there stood the most amazing structure.

Alice had never seen anything like it. It was taller than anything inside the dark and dusty floorboards, and covered in the most beautiful designs that reflected the red and rusty light of the afternoon sun.

"This is our crowning glory. My great great-grandfather spent a lifetime planning this and my father finished it many moons back. You will love it"

"What is it?" Alice asked.

The prince just smiled and led her towards the gigantic wooden doors. As they approached the doors swung open, as if by some sort of magical force.

Alice stepped through, and as she did, her jaw dropped. She stopped as still as the stone statues along the walls, unable to move or speak. There in front of her were row upon row of books, more than she ever expected to exist.

"How, where..."

She stuttered, unable to put a sentence together. "This is our library. All our knowledge and stories have been written down for everyone to enjoy. No one should be without knowledge and if anyone wants to learn then they are free to do so!"

"But how, how do I start…I never learned to read. My family forbade it."

"We will help you. Here in the library our wisest elders, from every species, are all here to help those who need it."

The prince led her towards a row of desks. Seated at each one was every type of creature, all dressed the same and all busy writing.

"This is Thomac."

The prince introduced Alice to a grasshopper. He was very quiet and moved with purpose.

"Hello Lady Alice, it is a pleasure to meet you."

She smiled at the word "Lady."

"I'm just Alice."

"Oh no, you're very special. We have not seen an albino spider for many moons."

"What do you mean? We have never been here, or I would have been told about this place."

"Oh, you have so much to learn."

The prince excused himself, saying he would return in time for the dinner bell, but for now he had to carry out his duties. Alice followed Thomac towards the rear of the library past rows upon rows of books. The scrolls called out to her.

"There is plenty of time for those. Right now I have something very important to show you."

Alice sat listening as Thomac ran through the history of the kingdom; how when it was first dreamed of there were seven tribes: the Wolf Spiders, the Grasshoppers, the Beetles, the Rats, the Moths and Butterflies, the Worms, and finally the Albino Spiders. She couldn't believe that her distant relatives had been part of this.

"What happened? Why did we leave?"

"That is a long story, one that will leave more questions than answers. I'm not sure that this is the time."

"Please Thomac, I need to know. The rest of my family is hiding away in the dark, scared to even think of the possibilities of the world outside."

Thomac cleared his throat.

"What I am about to tell you may not paint your family in a good light. I do not judge but this is what was written down by my predecessors."

"I'm ready! Please do tell!"

Many Moons Ago…

"We need to work together. That way we are stronger and can face any threat." Elrik stood trying to get everyone to calm down.

The council of seven were seated around a fire. Only the very first scratchings of any type of homes were around them; no walls, no library, no kingdom.

"The rats take more than their share!" shouted Zzkras, one of the council of seven.

"We bring in more." A fat old rat named Dami sat up from his lounging.

"That may be so, Dami, but we are doing the labour, the building, and the carrying." The voice came from an elderly looking wolf spider covered in grey fur. His voice carried an air of leadership and everyone listened.

"We get how your noses help find the best food, and we appreciate this, but my spiders and other creatures are all working from sunup to sunset to get things built, and we can't work without food."

Next to the wolf spider was the most beautiful albino spider, Queen Gabriella. Having only become queen several moons back she was still new to the ways of the seven. Her father had died during the winter, and she had not expected to become queen for many more moons. Her training was still ongoing, and she hated not being as forceful as the others.

"Please!" Gabriella spoke up. "Please, can we come to an agreement? We all need the shelter of the kingdom. The plan is for all of us to live together, but without a solid foundation this dream will end before it has begun."

The seven started talking amongst themselves. They would never get this to work if they could not even sort out the basics. Gabriella stood, excused herself and left. As she walked back to the albino spiders' camp, she wished her father was there to help guide her.

"Gabriella."

She stopped and turned around. There stood Dami. She was unsure about the rats. They did provide food for much of the populace, but they also seemed to look down at the other clans as if they were, somehow, better than the others.

"What can I do for you Dami? I'm tired and want to see my children before they go to sleep."

"We need to talk about the wolf spiders and how they want to rule this place."

"What makes you think they want to rule us? They have been as much a part of setting this up as anyone."

"They are plotting. They have ideas to make themselves the rulers!"

"But how do you know? What evidence do you have?"

"You will see. Don't say I didn't warn you."

With that Dami walked away and towards the rats' camp. They had set up in a burrow below ground. No one knew what was going on down there and if Gabriella didn't trust any of the other clans it would be the rats, with their secrets and hiding away in the dark.

Although she didn't trust Dami, she also had a feeling about the wolf spiders. The other creatures were all too weak to try to rule but Elrik and his clan could be strong enough if they tried. What was she going to do? She felt like she could trust no one. Entering their humble tent, she made her way to her corner to say goodnight to her children and think things over.

The following day as everyone went about their business, the burrowing creatures turned over the soil for planting. It was a task much needed to correct the damage done by man. Gabriella went to find the grasshoppers. Wise and long-lived, they planned things over many moons, not short-sighted like many of the creatures. She knew if anyone could help her it would be them.

When she arrived, she was surprised to see Dami there. Gabriella hid in the shadows unsure what the rat would be doing talking to the grasshoppers. Rats were far from religious and didn't need the guidance of anyone but their own.

The body language between them seemed aggravated. It was not a friendly chat but an argument. As Dami left she walked slowly towards the grasshoppers. Upon seeing her approach, Simon - a long-time family friend - came running out, grabbing her arm and leading her away.

"What's wrong?"

"You need to leave, quickly. Dami has told the other clans that you and your family are plotting to take control and that you plan to kill Elrik."

"What? That's crazy."

"I believe you, but until we can prove this you need to take your family and hide."

"Where should we go? We won't survive on our own."

"Get inside the old shop. There are tunnels and holes that you can use to hide. It won't be for long. I promise I will get the truth out of Dami, and we will meet again."

Gabriella ran.

"We need to leave and quickly!" she shouted, explaining as she packed. Others quickly started to help. They had never been under threat before, and this was scaring them all. Soon they had what little belongings they could carry and headed out across the fields towards mankind's long-abandoned shop. They were no more than halfway when shouts came echoing from the camp.

"Find the murderers!"

Murder! What was going on? Gabriella wanted to return but thought of her family,

"Run!" she shouted. "Get to the store and hide!"

"What about you?" one of Gabriela's nieces asked, she had a look of concern on her face, worried for the safety of her aunt and matriarch.

"I need to see what has happened. I need to clear our name."

Watching as her family disappeared into the night, she headed back towards the camp, unsure what was to greet her.

"Stop, murderer!"

She turned to find Dami and his guards blocking her escape. What did they mean, *murderer*? Then it all made sense. Dami had planned it all, to make her run, to set her up. But who had been killed?

9

Gabriella was taken in front of the five remaining clans. Elrik was not there and Dami had placed himself at the head, acting as leader and pushing his will onto the others.

"Gabriella, you have been brought here in front of the council to face the charges of murder. How do you plead?"

"This is madness! Can you not see that Dami set this up? He wants to control you all and is working to make us hate each other. He controls the food, and now he controls your minds."

Simon stood up and asked for silence as the rest of the council started bickering. They had all worked so hard to get this far. The madness was ripping them apart. They needed to see some sense in it all. He knew that Gabriella was innocent, but how to prove it?

"We need to have clear heads and hearts. This anger will only lead to division. Let's hear all sides before we make our decision."

They argued back and forth, over and over. No one could see any sense or no one wanted to. Dami and his lies had done the work, and the council was now on a path towards destruction.

As the sun set and the council retired for the night to consider their verdict, Simon went to see Gabriella hoping that there could be one last shot at righting this wrong.

"This isn't over. I will speak with the others. You and your family will be free to return, I promise."

"Thank you, Simon, but I fear it is too late for me. You can still help save my family. Find them in the old shop, tell them what happened, tell them to stay safe and to never trust anyone, apart from the grasshoppers. You have always been kind to us. We are being set up. Before long no one will remember the truth, and no one will care. We will be banished to the history books like tales of ghosts."

Simon bade his leave, promising that the truth would be recorded and one day the Albino clan would be welcomed back to the council and their rightful place in the kingdom.

Gabriella couldn't sleep. Thoughts of her family ran through her mind. Were they safe? Had Simon managed to warn them, and would they listen? She didn't care for her own life but the life of her children was the most important thing in the whole world for her.

At sunrise, the council gathered. Dami sat like the pretend ruler he was. To one side was Malon, Elrik's brother. He wasn't as level-headed as Elrik and was probably as power-hungry as Dami, but he would never resort to the underhanded tricks that the rats had to gain power.

"We are here to give verdict on the actions of the Albino clan and their leader Gabriella, and the charge of Murder."

The burrowers' leader Hayden stood. "We find Gabriella guilty."

Simon stood next. "Not guilty."

The Beetle's leader Zzkras: "Not guilty."

Dami did not even stand or make eye contact. "Guilty."

The leader from the flying creatures looked at the ground. They were the weakest of the clans, reliant on the most help from the others. "We find her guilty."

The last vote was the wolf spiders. Everyone looked at Malon; his vote would decide her fate. He could save her if he wanted to force a drawn court and make them all review their votes. She looked at his eyes, so alike the Wolf and Albino clans, but so different.

"Guilty."

"And that was how your family was expelled. I am so sorry, no one knew you had survived out there. Simon never let on what had happened, only writing these notes before he passed. Many moons came and went, and the Albino clan was all but forgotten, but now you're here, and we can help bring your family back to the kingdom."

Alice wasn't sure her family would see it like that. They had been in hiding so long that they had learned to fear the outside world.

"How has your day been?"

Alice turned as the prince came into the chamber. The emotions were flowing through her at the story she had been told; how the prince's long distant relative had given the final vote on the fate of Gabriella. How was she to move forward with this? She wanted her family here more than anything, but would the long distant choices of the past come back and condemn them all?

She ran past the prince, unable to talk to him right then. She needed space from everything she had been told and seen; the great library and its many secrets, the hatred caused by the rats and the belief that Gabriella had been behind Elrik's murder.

What was she to do? She no longer had family near her. The burden of the secret she had learned caused her to cry as she ran, exactly as she had done at the beginning of her crazy adventure. Was she running away from everything again? She stopped. It was time to stop running to face up to the challenges and make things right.

She turned back to the library, knowing what she needed to do. That's when they struck, three huge rats, covered in scars and armour, grabbing her. They pinned her to the floor, then a fourth rat came from the shadows. She recognised its face, the snarl and its teeth.

"What do you want? Let me go!"

"Oh, not this time little one. There is no prince here to save you. There is someone who wants to speak with you."

At that, she was struck on the head, knocking her out.

Alice came round. Her head hurt and she felt sick. Then she remembered what had happened, turning quickly to see where she was; too quickly, making the room spin.

It was a dark, damp room, obviously underground, but she could not tell more.

"Ah, you're awake."

She turned at the voice. It was the same rat as before, the one who had tried to kill her and now taken her captive.

"The less you struggle, the quicker this will go."

Two other rats approached her. She went to run, but again the room spun. Tripping as the chain on her legs tightened, sending her crashing to the damp, slimy floor.

"Stop struggling. The elder wants to see you and once he is done you will be mine, and I haven't eaten a spider for many moons."

Dragging her from her cell, along the dark, smelly tunnels, she saw hundreds of rats, all watching as she was pulled along.

"I can't believe it's true! When I was told about an albino spider, I thought they must be telling me lies. The albinos died out, whilst exiled from the kingdom in the very beginning after I had Gabriella executed for her part in the murder of Elrik."

"Gabriella did not kill anyone!"

"Oh, so you've heard the story of the kingdom. Have you heard all of it, though?"

Alice looked at the rat in front of her. It could not be the same rat, that was so many moons ago.

"What do you know of those times? The only records are in the library and I doubt very much you can read."

Alice laughed at the hideous old rat in front of her, trying to delay the inevitable.

"I don't need to read the story. I lived it. I was there. My name is Dami, I am the first great rat and the leader of this clan and rightful king of the lands above. One day soon I will take it from the bugs and insects, and they will all serve us as their masters."

"I don't believe you; no one is that old, not even my grandmother."

"Ah, so there are more of you. I thought you had all died out in the wilderness, when Gabriella sent her family away. I should have hunted you down then and finished the job.

if Gabriella and Elrik had joined together like their hearts wanted, then they would have been too powerful. I could not allow that, so I put into action plans to have them split for eternity. But it seems that fate has a very funny sense of humour and has bought the Albino and Wolf clans back together."

Alice couldn't believe it. Was this the case? Was this really Dami? She needed to get away to warn her family.

"Take her away! Find out where the rest of her clan is hiding. We will hunt them down and kill them all!"

"Please, let me go home. I'll never speak of this. My family wouldn't want to come here anyway. They're scared of everything."

"I can't risk that, little one. I will make sure it is quick, and they do not suffer. So just tell us where they are or you will SUFFER."

They took her back to the damp cell. Alice knew she had to do something to warn everyone of the plan that Dami had for the kingdom.

"Father, have you seen Alice anywhere?"

"No, why do you ask, son? What is it?"

"She spent the day in the library and when I arrived to collect her for supper she was upset and ran off. I have searched everywhere, but she's vanished."

"Why was she upset? What did that old fool Simon tell her?"

As the king finished his question, the door to the royal chambers opened and Simon walked in.

"Sir, I have grave news."

"What is it? What did you tell Lady Alice?"

"Sir, I believe she has been taken. It's my fault, sir."

Simon explained about the scroll, the story of the kingdom, and how Alice had run away when the prince arrived, presumably because she was worried she would be blamed for what happened all those years ago.

"I have asked around, and some children reported seeing rats, sir, in the daylight by the kingdoms walls. They hadn't said anything as they also were outside the walls and were afraid they would be in trouble." Simon looked concerned, if he had looked after Alice, this would not have happened.

"Father, we need to get her back. This is my fault! I should have taken more care of her!"

"If she is related to Gabriella, then we need to correct the wrongs of the past. Malon should have listened to his heart, but he was greedy for power and that is not our way. Assemble the guards."

"Sir, can I offer caution? If we head to the tunnels, the rats will have the advantage, and we will be trapped in very close quarters. We should draw them out, into the open, where our numbers will have an advantage over their strength." One of the princes closest and trusted friends stood by, offering his advice and guidance.

"How do you mean? What would make them leave the tunnels?"

"The dam, sir, we breach it and flood the tunnels. The rats will come out, and we can then rescue Alice."

"It's risky. What if they leave her to die?"

"I don't think they will. They want to end not just her life but all the albino spiders. I think the rats fear a union between the albinos and the wolf spiders."

"They will want to know where the rest of her family is and kill them all. She'll be safe until then."

"Sir, we can't risk that many soldiers, leaving the kingdom unguarded. I have a better idea. I will take a handful of soldiers, a small raiding party, enough to fight if need be, but small enough to sneak past their guards."

The king agreed, and the prince ran to set things in motion.

Alice was close to giving up. She was hurting all over where the rats cut her, beat her and threatened her, but she kept going, keeping strong for her family, knowing she would never forgive herself if they were killed.

Hours later she sat quietly, bound and beaten, on the cold, damp floor. Not letting the hurt show to her tormentors, she kept telling herself she needed to escape to let everyone know what happened all those years back; to stop Dami and his evil army of rats from destroying everything.

The door to her cell opened. She could smell him before she saw him: Dami had come personally this time. This was not good. So far, he'd kept his distance, instructing his minions to do the dirty work. Alice guessed he was getting desperate, wanting answers she was not willing to give.

"It's your final chance. Tell me what I want to know, and this can end quickly, or today will be so filled with pain and hurt that even if you tell me, it will be harder for you."

"Why do you hate us so much? What did we do to you?"

"Oh, you are so young, and obviously you haven't been told the truth, how Gabriella kept us rats at the bottom of the pile. We did all the work, and she acted like a queen, and that is exactly what she wanted to do, be queen and rule everyone."

"Liar! I have been told the story that you didn't want to be an equal, you wanted it all to yourself, the kingdom, the food, everything; to be in charge to be lording it over the others."

"Do you think the scrolls you have been shown hold the truth? That was many moons ago, and I am the only one left from that time, so don't you think that I would know?"

"I think you would say anything to get me to talk, but it won't work."

Dami swung out at Alice, striking her hard and knocking the wind from her. As she lay on the floor gasping for breath, Dami approached, drawing a blade from his belt. This was going to be the end. She said silent goodbyes to her family, begging their forgiveness for running away, for if she had listened to her father, stayed safe in their little world, this would not be happening to her. But then she would not know the story of her family, the magnificence of the world outside. The blade rose above her, and she shut her eyes.

A scream came from outside the cell, and then another. She opened her eyes. Dami stood there above her, paused in his deadly task.

"Guards, Guards!"

"Your precious guards are busy."

Alice turned towards the door and there stood the prince. He was cut and bloodied, but he had come. Dami, snarled showing his broken yellow teeth.

"You think you can stop me, you pathetic little spider?"

"I don't need to stop you; I am just here to take lady Alice back."

"Then you will need to go through me!"

Dami lunged at the prince, but the prince dived, swinging his spear. The fight became a blur as the two danced a dangerous dance.

The prince swung hard at Dami, striking the rat and sending him flying through the air, smashing into an old upright. Rubble fell to the floor from tunnel roof. The prince ran to Alice and started to cut her bonds. She was nearly free.

Dami had made his way to his feet and ran at them.

"Look out!"

The prince turned as Dami was on the prince, ripping at him.

The prince screamed out in pain as Dami ripped one of his legs clean off. Alice looked on in terror. She had never seen such brutality.

Dami was now on top of the prince, clawing and scratching, dripping drool as he spoke.

"You dare to face me alone and think you can stop me?"

Alice struck as hard as she could with the spear. She had never carried out such violence and felt awful for doing so but her friend was going to be killed.

The spear dug into Dami and he cried out in pain. Turning towards Alice as she backed away, he crawled forwards, blood pouring from the wound in his side. He jumped at her, striking out with his claws, but Alice dived to the side. Dami crashed into the wall, and this time the ceiling did not hold. Dozens of rocks came crashing down on him.

Alice looked towards the prince. He was losing blood and looked in a bad way. She called for help. Had the prince really come alone? She called again but this time two of the palace guards appeared. Lifting the prince up, they carried him from the tunnels and back to the kingdom.

Alice sat by the prince's side. The grasshoppers treated his wound and stopped the bleeding, but he was not in the clear yet. His wounds were deep and the blood loss great. Alice sat and stayed, watching as the prince lay there fighting for his life.

The king stood in the doorway, quietly talking to Simon. After all that had happened, the reason why Alice had run away and the story of the torture she had been through at the hands of Dami, the king knew he had to make things right. The rats' lies and deceit from many moons ago had destroyed so much.

He coughed gently so that Alice knew he was there.

"Your highness." She curtsied.

"Please." He gestured for her to sit back down. "You are like family; my son obviously likes you."

Alice blushed.

"Please tell me all that you know, from the beginning."

The king sat and listened, and Alice spoke of her family, of where she lived and how she had been told of the past and Gabriella, and the way the rats had tried to control the kingdom.

As she finished her story the king sighed a deep and thoughtful sigh.

"We need to get your family and bring them here. Dami may be dead but there are other rats, those who've waited for the day that Dami passed to make their own attempt at power."

The prince moaned in his sleep. Sweat clung to his brow, and he looked in pain. Alice wiped at his brow and started to sing a soothing song from her home, the one that her granny had always sung to her when she was ill. As she sung, the king looked on, amazed, for he knew the song. It had been sung to him by his grandparents, and they had always said it was passed to them by their grandparents. The song had gone full circle and had come home.

Over the days the prince grew stronger. He was still sore where his leg had been so violently removed, but he was getting used to moving around without it. He and Alice spent most of the time together, Alice encouraging him to move, to get his strength back and the prince happy to keep her near so no harm could come to her.

As the new moon rose, the king and queen came to them. They had news from their spies within the rats' kingdom.

"It seems there was a power struggle. Several of the more powerful rats have been killed and alliances have changed. As the dust settled, though, there was a final battle within their walls and—" The king paused, unsure how to break the news.

"What is it, Father?"

"It's Dami. He was found alive under the rubble. He is in a bad way but is gaining strength. A few of his more devote followers have run to his side, and he has enough warriors to keep control, for now."

"How can that be? He was squashed, stabbed and beaten." the prince looked concerned at the news of Dami's continued reign.

"I know, Son, but this has come from a very reliable source, and if he gets his full strength back then we will be in for a fight. We need allies. The bugs and worms will stand with us, the grasshoppers will advise us, but we need more."

He turned to Alice, a look of pleading in his eyes.

"Would you return home, bring your family here? All of them, every single able-bodied spider. We need them. If we fall, Dami will come for you and your family, and then we will all be his slaves."

She couldn't believe what she was being asked. Her family had been hiding in isolation for so long, for them to even consider leaving their little world was incomprehensible. Alice had been the first to leave that sanctuary.

"I... I don't know if they will. We have lived alone for so long, being told stories to keep us hidden, with stories passed down from generation to generation. I don't know if I alone can convince them."

"You won't be alone."

The prince stood up and hobbled towards the king.

"I will escort Lady Alice. I will ensure she is safe, and then we will speak to her elders and convince them that they will be safer here."

"Are you sure? Your strength is not fully regained and if there is trouble on the way, what will you do?"

"I will protect him." Alice held a steadfast look, determined in this quest. "We will have each other's back."

"I cannot spare many guards. One or two at most, maybe. If Dami attacks, I need every able-bodied creature we have."

"We'll be fine, Father. I will take a couple of my men, enough to defend ourselves, and escort the rest of the albinos back here to safety."

"Okay. You leave at dusk."

The king left the two young spiders alone. Alice looked at the prince and then at his wound. Would he be able to make the climb up to the ceiling? Could she even remember the way back?

What would her family think, they may not even believe her and the amazing story that she had to tell?

Dami stood in the great hall of his lair. There in front of him knelt three traitors. They had been seen heading to the kingdom above and followed the rat who had reported it. The rat stood to one side, explaining that he had seen them talking to a spider; he had overheard them telling all.

"What do you say to these accusations?"

"You want to end it all. Above ground, they have everything: food, clean water, peace, but all you want is chaos."

"I want to rule like I was meant to all those years back, and dirty backstabbing rats like you will not stop me."

He nodded at a large black rat standing to one side. Adus had been loyal to Dami for many moons, protecting him against others.

Adus drew a large blade and ran the first rat through.

"Please sir, I have information!" the second rat begged.

"And what information is that?"

"The prince! He and the albino will be heading into the shop, back to lady Alice's home. They are going to rally more troops from the Albino clan."

"Ah, interesting...tell me more."

The rat talked and talked, telling all he had learnt from his trips to the kingdom, until Dami seemed satisfied.

"I'm sorry sir, please forgive me."

"You are forgiven."

Dami nodded again at Adus who swung his blade, ending the rat's life. He swung again, and the final traitor was slain. Dami turned away.

"We need to move and fast. Take your best men, cut off the prince and find these albino spiders. Kill every single, last one and then end that prince once and for all. But bring the girl back here, she is mine."

"Yes sir."

Adus left the hall, wiping the blood from his sword. He would enjoy this hunt, he loved nothing more than a fresh kill, and the prince needed to be ended in the most painful way.

The going was slow. The prince struggled with each step. Two of his friends volunteered to come along and the four of them walked in silence. Alice looked for clues to help her remember the way. The prince had told them how to get to the room and up to the vent on the roof where he had kept watch that very first night. The climb up was hard, with the prince's friends taking turns to support him. Alice led the way climbing the walls of the old bookshop. The paint peeled off and dust choked them as they went but onwards and upwards they climbed.

It was early morning when they reached the roof. The sun was just breaking the horizon, its orange red glow bathing the four in its warmth. As they set up camp so that the prince could rest, Alice climbed to the highest point she could find.

Upon reaching the very tip of a spire, she looked out. The sun, now higher in the sky, cast long, dark shadows across the ground. Nearby she could see the cleared land of the kingdom, and nearer the building were fields of rubble and rubbish left by mankind. Funny, she thought; the name *mankind*! For the stories she had been told did not paint them as kind. They had hunted and killed, and they polluted and destroyed the very land that kept them alive.

She could see further still and then the devastation. There were no trees, just small scrub-type bushes, scorched bits of ground where nothing grew. What had man done to the Earth? A tear formed in her eyes as she looked around at the complete devastation. If only man had looked after the Earth, then it would have looked after them.

"Hey, are you OK?"

She turned to see one of the prince's friends, Tobi, standing there.

"The prince sent me to keep watch."

"I'm fine, just enjoying the sun. I'm not sure when I will see it again once we head inside."

"You should head down. Food will be ready soon, and we need to rest before the final stretch."

She nodded and turned to look one more time at the sun and surrounding lands, promising herself that she would return, she would bring her family, and they too would enjoy all that the lands could give.

They sat around the camp, eating fresh fruit, chatting and laughing like it was a normal day out with friends. Tobi, told stories of the prince when he was younger and how they had always gotten into trouble. The prince blushed at stories of his past attempts to win the affection of girls.

Alice told stories of growing up in the dark and the stories her grandparents had told to keep them safe. As she recalled them, she wondered what must have happened to them on the way from the kingdom to scare them so much that they did not want to return.

She would find out one day, but now was not the time. They had one task, to get to her family before it was too late and bring them home to the kingdom.

Later that day, standing by the crack in the plaster and the entrance to Alice's world, they stepped through into the darkness beyond and all turned to look at the sunlight one last time.

"I know you were running when you found your way out, but do you have any clue which way to go?"

Alice looked around, searching for something, anything, that could be of help, but there was nothing. It all looked the same. Then she caught sight of the marks, little splatters in the dust, made from her tears.

"This way!"

Setting off, she led them into the darkness, homeward-bound.

They followed the trail, sometimes having to stop and check the branches of the tunnels as they went, and slowly found their way deeper into the darkness. The prince and his friends struggled to adjust to the pitch-black gloom. Alice kept them going, her eyes working as they were designed to do when growing up in the dark.

"We must be close, look!"

She pointed at the wall. There was some spider silk made into a makeshift sign. At the next junction she recognised the small house. It belonged to a hermit who was said to be older than all the elders together, but no one believed it, it was just another story to entertain the children. But Alice now thought this could be also been true. So much had changed since she had first set foot into the world beyond the floorboards. What else was true? If Dami was that old, why could there not be a spider the same age?

"Wait here," she said.

She walked up to the door and knocked gently. There was no answer. Strange, she thought, although he lived alone, he would always welcome visitors. Knocking again, this time a little harder, she found still no answer. She turned to her friends and beckoned them over.

"What's wrong, who lives here?"

"Just an old hermit. He kept to himself but would always welcome a visitor."

"Let me try."

The prince stepped forward and knocked, a firm but friendly knock, but still no answer. He tried the handle and the door swung open. Inside was a mess. Odd little trinkets lay across the floor, a chair was knocked over and there was food on the little hearth, boiling over the edge of a pot.

"Hello?"

The prince stepped in, signalling for the others to wait.

"Hello, is anyone here?"

He slowly walked through the hallway, stepping over the bits and bobs on the floor.

Reaching a door, he drew his spear and pushed it open slowly. He could see more mess with a bed unmade and more belongings strewn across the floor...but nothing else.

"There's no one here!" he called.

"This is strange. He had his food delivered and I can't remember the last time he left his house."

"We need to keep going to find your parents and the rest of your clan."

Alice hurried from the tiny little house. The others followed behind. They struggled to keep up as she ran, panicking at thought of her family being in danger.

They approached the edge of the town, and became cautious at the strange silence that surrounded them. Alice stopped and pointed at the house ahead of them.

"That's my house, but something's wrong. My dad would never leave the window open and the fire on." She pointed at the smoke coming from the tiny chimney.

"Spread out!" the prince instructed his friends.

"We will approach the front, as if returning home. You two flank us. At any sign of danger we head back to the hermit's house."

Alice and the prince walked towards the house. It was still too quiet. Even early in the morning there would be others going about their business; the baker opening up his shop with fresh bread, others heading out to forage...something was wrong.

They were no more than halfway when a shout came from Alice's house.

"Run Alice, save yourself!"

It was her mum. Alice went to run towards the house, but the prince grabbed her.

"No, it's a trap!"

"But that's my mum!"

"I know, but we need to get the others."

"Run!" The shout was cut short, followed by a scream and then a thud.

The door to the little cottage swung open. Out stepped a rat so huge he broke the door frame as he pushed through it. Alice had never seen anything so big and ugly. It was even bigger than Dami and looked ten times stronger.

"My name is Adus. I am the general of King Dami's army. He sent me on a special mission, one that you will not enjoy but I will!"

"Let my mum go! Where is everyone else, my brother, my father and grandmother?"

"Don't worry, little girl, they won't suffer for much longer! Unlike you!"

The way Adus said that, Alice knew they would not be okay for long. But what could she do? They would probably not be able to defeat Adus, and she guessed he wasn't alone.

"What do you want?"

"Oh, just the death of your friends, and to take you back to Dami."

The prince moved forward, putting himself between Alice and Adus.

"How about you and me? If I win, your soldiers, who are no doubt hiding, must leave, and never come back!" the prince shouted across to the rat.

"If you win!" Adus laughed "You have only seven legs and are weaker than the smallest ladybug. Why would I waste my time?"

"Sounds like you are scared!"

The prince taunted Adus, hoping this would distract him enough. He had seen his two friends flanking the house looking for the other rats that no doubt hid nearby. They had made it to Alice's home and had sneaked in behind Adus.

"So Fatty Ratty, what's it going to be?" he asked, doing all he could to get Adus to move forward and further away from the house.

"I haven't time for this, boy!"

Adus turned back to the house just as Tobi came out with Alice's brother.

"What!" Adus screamed. He drew his sword and charged at Tobi, who dived to the side. Tobi was one of the most skilled warriors in the kingdom. He drew his own sword and parried the rats' strikes, one after another. The rat had the upper hand with height and strength, but Tobi was fast, jumping and diving again and again. He managed to strike the rat several times but still Adus came at him. The prince charged to join the fight.

Alice started to skirt around, making her way to the house, hoping the back door was unguarded. Finding the door open, she slowly entered her home. It was strangely quiet. Where was her father and the rest of her family?

She went room to room searching for any sign of them, but there was none. She was about to give up when she noticed that her mother's coffee table was not in the normal place, and neither was the rug. She walked towards them trying to figure what had been done. As she stepped onto the rug, the floor gave way, and she fell through into the darkness below.

Alice and her brother had often hidden down here, trying to scare the adults above. She hid here alone after being berated by her father, so she knew where the passage led. Had the rest of her family used the tunnels to hide and escape? Were they alive? She dared to hope.

The thought of finding her family dead sent a shiver down her spine. Her mum was upstairs. Hopefully the prince or one of his friends had moved her aside. As Tobi had tried to stop Adus, she heard her brother as they were escorted away from the property. But there was still no sign of the others.

She heard a crash upstairs. The fight was now inside the little house. She popped her head out of the hole and watched as Tobi was thrown across the living room and crashed into the little table. Adus was on him in a flash and Tobi seemed to be losing. Suddenly the door swung open and the prince ran in, his blade held aloft he launched himself at the rat.

Alice dived back into the hole. She was not getting back out the way she came in, and she still needed to find the rest of her family. She headed along the passage; if her family had escaped, it would be to go this way. The passage twisted and turned, and she run with purpose, hoping that she was not too late.

She came to a small room. In the far corner was a hatch and as she hoped it was unlocked but closed. She opened it slowly, whispering for her father. But there was no answer. This time she called a little louder and was pleased to hear a voice call back.

"Alice, is that you?"

"Granny?"

From the dark and gloom her grandma appeared, a smile on her face that soon turned to sadness.

"What is it?"

"Were you followed? How did you get past the rats...? Your mum and brother, where are they?"

"They are safe, they are with friends."

"Friends, or more strangers in our town?"

"These aren't like the rats, they are...well you will have to see. Is my father here?"

Her granny stood quietly, unsure how to answer. The look on her face grew sadder, a look of sorrow said it all. Alice collapsed to the floor.

Her gran climbed out of the hole and gently touched Alice's shoulder to comfort her.

"The rats came last night. Your father stood his ground and gave us time to get away. Your mum hid the entrance, but your brother had hidden in the house too scared to leave without them. Your father he was so brave, but they cut him down."

Alice sat and stared at the floor. She had caused this. By running away the rats had found out about them. She killed her father.

"I know what you are thinking," her grandmother said in a calm voice, "but this is not your fault."

"It is, though. If I hadn't run away then this would never have happened."

"No, that is not the truth little one. Please do not blame yourself for this. We've hidden here for so many moons, the rats would have found us eventually. I am surprised it didn't happen sooner."

"You knew of the rats? Why didn't you tell us? Who else knew?"

Alice felt relief but also betrayal at the same time. Did everyone know about the rats? She couldn't get her thoughts together. She couldn't figure out why they didn't warn her against going anywhere. Yes, she'd wanted to read, but not at the risk of her family and friends.

"There will be time for questions, but right now we need to catch up with your mother and brother."

Alice stood. She had lost her father, but she would not let harm come to anyone else.

The battle was brutal. Dozens of rats attacked the three warriors. The prince struggled to fight because of his injury, but he knew he could count on his friends defending and parrying each attack.

Adus had long fled the fight, realising that they had bitten off more than they could chew. He ordered his soldiers to stay and fight, and they would never question him or his bravery.

Alice and the rest of her family cautiously approached the square of the little hamlet. She couldn't believe the sight: dead and wounded rats lay everywhere. She looked for the prince, a smile creeping on to her face as she saw him resting against a wall across from the battlefield. To his side, his friends rested. They also looked worn-out, cut and bloodied, but alive.

She gestured to her family to follow her towards the strangers. She could hear them whisper, scared of these large brown spiders, of what had happened in their little town. In hundreds of moons, nothing had ever threatened their home. Rats had now attacked, and strange brown spiders had come from nowhere, bringing Alice home.

"Lady Alice!" The prince hobbled towards her, a smile on his face.

"Prince Tellon, you're hurt?"

"It's nothing, I... We will all be fine."

Alice looked round at the group of friends, pleased that no one else had died due to her stupidity. She turned to her family.

"This is my grandma, and the rest of our family."

"You have your grandfather's looks." Alice's grandmother stepped forward and curtsied to the prince.

"Please, there is no need for that. How did you know my grandfather?"

"Not in person, but I had heard stories when I was Alice's age until the elders forbid all talk of the kingdom and the world outside. For now, we need to gather the others along with supplies and head to the kingdom. We need to warn the king. The rats won't take this lightly and I expect they will plan on making a move to rule the kingdom."

Alice stood in shock. All this time her granny had known, was that why she had encouraged her to be more than just a spider. She knew that one day the little underground world of the albinos and the kingdom outside would need to reunite and that the albino and wolf spiders would need to work together for the greater good.

A noise from her left startled Alice. Turning, she smiled as her brother and mother came out of hiding. She ran over to them with tears in her eyes and a sick feeling in the pit of her stomach at the thought of her father being killed by the rats.

"I'm so sorry!" Alice cried, hugging her mum.

"It's okay, don't blame yourself. Your father was always hard on you, but he loved you and would never let anything happen to you or your brother."

Suddenly a scream from the gathered spiders drew their attention. A wounded rat had grabbed the old hermit, holding the elderly spider tightly, edging towards the wall and its way back to the rats' lair.

"Let him go!"

Alice stepped forward, standing tall and promising herself not to show fear.

"Let him go and you might live."

"Ha! Why would I trust you and your kind? All the albino spiders ever did was stab everyone in the back."

"What do you mean?"

"You must know the stories of Gabriella and her attempt to take over the kingdom."

"They are lies, made up by your leader, in his failed attempt to take control of the kingdom."

"Don't be absurd. You have always been the problem!"

As the rat shouted, his broken yellow teeth dripped saliva over the old hermit's hair. A spear came from nowhere, striking the rat square in the face, killing him instantly.

Alice turned to her granny who stood proudly, having thrown the spear from 30 yards away. Alice could not believe her eyes.

"How?"

"There will be time for questions. Let's move."

The troop of spiders and their new friends made their way back towards the wide world beyond the walls and the waiting kingdom. Nerves were high and many of the elder spiders were worried about leaving the safety of their village. Questions buzzed around.

"What if we don't make it?"

"What will happen to our homes?"

"Why should we trust these outsiders?"

"You can trust them. They saved me more than once and if they had not come back with me, you would all be slaves to the rats or worse."

"But if you had not left in the first place we would have never been found by the rats."

"Oh, poppycock!" Alice's gran shouted.

"The elders knew the truth. I remember the stories we were told, of Gabriella and the exodus from the kingdom. Yes, we may have forgotten over time, but that doesn't make it any less real."

Her gran stopped in her tracks, turning to the others, and stood straight, straighter than Alice had seen in a long time. She held an air of authority and a determined look in her eye.

"We need to believe in this. We need to stop living in the dark and go back to the world. The kingdom was going to be part of our lives. We would have been involved in its birth and seen it grow into the wonder that it is now."

Without waiting for any comments from the others, she turned and marched on.

The spiders breached into the store through the little hole that Alice had found not that long back, and as each one stepped through, they all had the same look of wonder and surprise on their faces. Some looked a little scared, but for most of them, this was the biggest adventure of their lives.

Alice's gran stepped through last, and stopped on the edge and looked in wonder. The world was bigger than she had ever imagined. She'd often felt jealous of Alice and her youth. Alice had time to make more of her life than she had. She had a chance to actually see the world and that's why she had filled her granddaughter's head with dreams and stories, hoping that she would take the chance to do exactly what she had wanted.

Now she was also living this dream to experience the adventure, she knew she had not much time left. She was already older than most spiders they knew and really didn't expect to be leaving her home at this time of life.

Stopping for the night to give everyone chance to rest, Alice was itching to leave. She paced around the small camp, keeping a watch on the little ones and making sure everyone had been fed.

"How are you doing?"

Alice turned at the prince's voice, a flush of red on her cheeks. Since the battle they had not had a chance to talk. All the young spiderlings wanted to hear of the prince's adventures and the elders wanted to know of the kingdom. Now they had their fill of stories and adventures and were settling down for the night.

"Let's take a walk"

The prince took Alice's arm, heading up along the wall and through the same broken window Alice had gone through that very first night he had seen her.

"I saw you, when you first came out here. I was unsure if you were a friend or foe or even a ghost with that bright white fur."

"A ghost, there's no such thing." Alice laughed.

"Are you so sure?" the prince teased.

They walked to the little pipe where Alice had slept that night and sat watching the moon rise into the star-filled sky.

"Some stories in the library say that mankind left the earth in great ships after they poisoned the ground, the water and the very air they breathed. Other stories say that they all died out when the earth could no longer support them, and the last one left was a young girl. Left alone after her father died a few years before, she wandered the earth salvaging what she could. Finally, with the last of her energy she collapsed on the very ground out there."

The prince waved at the rubble-strewn ground below them. From this high Alice was still amazed by the view. These were distances beyond her wildest dreams. What other amazing places were out there? Were there other kingdoms, or worse, were there more hordes of rats?

Her attention was bought back to the present as the prince continued his story.

"As she lay there, the creatures and bugs approached her cautiously, for they had heard of the greed of men. Realising she was just a young girl, and that she had not caused the devastation but had been a victim of her own elders' greed and selfishness, the creatures bought her food and water. Slowly she regained her strength, and finally when she was strong enough, she thanked all the creatures. Making her own house, she set about helping them to grow food from the seeds they had and found ways for them to store water, then finally teaching her new friends how to build dwellings from stones and sticks.

"Decades later, when she was much older, knowing it was her time to pass onto the next world, she lay down, giving her body to the earth so that plants and trees could grow from the very body that they had helped survive. That girl's name was Eden and this is her garden, exactly where the kingdom is built."

The prince finished his story, turning to Alice, who had a dream-like look on her face.

"But that's just a story, isn't it?"

"Isn't the story of Gabriella in the same library?"

They sat and watched the moon move across the sky, Alice feeling safe for the first time in a long time, cuddled up in the prince's arms.

Continuing their journey across the wasteland, between the old bookshop and the kingdom, was slower than Alice liked. The older spiders needing to rest; the younger spiders wanting to investigate everything and running off all the time.

"We are less than a day's travel now to the kingdom. The borders are near!"

The prince shouted so that the whole group could hear him. This gave everyone strength at the thought of being at the end of this great journey, but now there were grumbles. Why had they left their home? What if the kingdom refused them entry? The prince and Alice did their best to calm their nerves and to keep the group moving towards its final goal.

Sending his friends ahead to warn the guards that they would be coming, the prince stood with a proud look on his face. He knew that there was work to be done. Houses would need to be built, and the albinos would need time to settle in, but there was time for that.

The smile fell from his face at the thought of the rats and their plan to dominate all the creatures. The sooner he could inform the king of these plans, the sooner they could take the initiative and stop them.

With less than half a day's travel left, Alice relaxed a little. They had outrun the rats, and escorted her family and friends to safety. She wished her father was here to see this. He would have been speechless at what Alice, the little albino spider, had achieved, but she knew he would have been so proud.

Tears formed in her eyes at the thought of her father. She stopped looking back the way they had come, back towards the shop along with its dust-covered shelves and the endless rows of books, and hidden away in the dark musky space between its floorboard, the tiny little place they had called home.

They hadn't had time to search for her father's corpse or give him a proper burial. She picked a small flower from their garden and placed on the doorstep of their home.

She promised herself she would get the grasshoppers to write her father's story so that future generations knew how they had come to be here in the kingdom.

Staring at the place they had come from, her eyes caught sight of movement. In the distance, a great plume of dust rose into the air. She focused on what was causing such a disturbance. At first, she thought it was a large creature, which would have been strange since as far as she knew most large mammals had died out.

Then she made out shapes. It wasn't one creature, it was hundreds; hundreds of rats, and at the front was Dami.

"Run!" Alice shouted as loudly as she could.

The group stopped and looked at her, confused by this sudden shout of fear.

"Run now!"

This time pushing those closest to her, Alice urged them on.

"The rats are coming! Move now, leave everything!"

The group started to move, but not fast enough. Alice shouted again.

"Move, come on!"

Wanting them to move quicker still, if the rats caught them they would all be slaughtered. None would be spared and then the kingdom would fall as well.

"We need them to hurry."

Turning to the prince, Alice was scared. She thought they were safe and that she would be able to save her family and friends, but now seeing the horde of rats advancing on them, she had a feeling that she had failed.

"What do we do? There is no way we can make it!"

"Go, lead your people home!" The prince readied himself, drawing his sword with a steadfast look on his face.

"You can't fight them all!"

"I don't need to; I just need to defeat Dami."

Alice looked at the prince and then at his missing leg from the last encounter with the rats.

"You nearly died last time, and you had all your limbs then. There is no way that you will be able to beat him."

"I have to try!"

Alice looked at the group. Most had run, following the path. Some stood in fear crying. She didn't know what to do.

"Go save them!"

Turning to the remaining spiders, she screamed, "Run! Follow the path and keep going!"

She turned to her brother. "Run ahead, catch up with the prince's friends, get to the kingdom and tell them we need help."

"What are you doing?" the prince shouted. "You need to leave!"

"No, this time I'm with you."

"So am I."

They turned to see Alice's granny standing there, with a don't-mess-with-me look on her face.

"Please, I can't see you two die for nothing."

"Three."

Alice's mum stepped forward, then more and more of the albino spiders, all those able and fit enough forming a ragtag army.

Alice encouraged the others, those unable to fight to keep going. If they could buy enough time maybe they would make it behind the walls of the kingdom.

The small group of spiders searched for stones, sticks, anything that could be used as a weapon. With the narrow path maybe they could hold them off, but it wouldn't be for long.

The rats were now moments away, at least 200 of them, all angry, showing their yellow teeth with a look of bloodlust and hatred in their eyes.

Alice looked at the prince. She wanted to tell him how she felt, but that would distract him from his task. With a feeling in her gut that this would be the last time she would have the chance, she turned to the little group of spiders, trying to encourage them and hoping that her words would give them strength to see this through.

The prince hoped that Dami would allow one-on-one combat, but the rats could never be trusted. If any of them tried to sneak by they would have to come through the gorge and this little group of spiders would do all that they could to stop them.

As they drew nearer, Alice could smell the stench coming from the horde. She had never seen so many creatures in one place. The noise and the smell were overpowering.

The prince stepped forward and stood defiantly. With his spear and armour on, he looked like a magnificent warrior. The first rats were nearly on him. As they pounced, he swung his spear, and two – no, three – lay dead. The rats kept coming and the prince kept swinging.

Finally, Dami appeared. He had deliberately sent his soldiers forward to weaken the prince and now as he stood on top of the dead and dying rats, he looked down at the prince.

"So little boy, you have come back for more, have you? How about this time I take your life not just your limb!" There on his belt hung the prince's severed leg, like some sort of bloodied trophy.

"I will not let you harm anyone else. These spiders are under the protection of the kingdom. I command you to go back to your lair and leave this ground."

Dami laughed and turned to his army.

"What do you say to that?"

The rats cheered in defiance, edging forward. Some even threw spears and stones and at the small spider army standing behind the prince.

"Well, I guess we won't be doing as you command."

"I challenge you then to single combat, as per the rules set out when the kingdom was first dreamt of."

The prince hoped that Dami would still honour this outdated and little-known rule from many moons ago. No one had issued a challenge in such a long time, but there was still an order to things that all creatures should follow.

Dami looked worried, and showed a momentary flash of fear. The prince was skilled and a great deal younger than Dami, and he himself was old and tired, but he could not back down in front of his men. They would soon lose trust in their leader, and he would face being removed one way or another.

"You have to accept the challenge, sir!"

Adus stood to the side, still trying to regain face after he lost the battle at the albino spider village.

"How dare he tell me what to do? You failed me, and now you dare dictate to me!"

Dami swung out with his blade and Adus fell to the ground.

"I accept your challenge, boy, but just so you know I will win, and once I am finished with you, I will round up your friends, and they will die a slow horrible death. And once I am finished with them, I will continue to the kingdom and claim the throne for myself from your father! I may even let him live long enough to see his family destroyed."

"You have to win first, and I do not plan on letting you!"

The prince took off his helmet and armour. They would protect him from some blows, but he would be quicker without them. He turned to Alice, smiled and charged.

The two danced a deadly dance, each taking blows and each striking the other. Alice could hardly watch as the prince swung his spear, trying with all his might to land a fatal blow. Dami fought back, his eyes red with rage, trying his best to pin the prince and using his tail as a whip. A number of times he pulled one of the prince's legs from under him, but each time the prince sprang to his feet, ready to counter the attacks.

A scream drew Alice's attention, and turning, she saw her mum backing away from a rat that had tried to flank the group. Alice's gran threw a rock at the rat. Again her aim was true and she struck the rat between the eyes, making it retreat. Other rats had started to move on the group. They readied themselves for their own fight. The rats had not expected any of their targets to strike back and seeing Alice's gran strike one of their comrades had made them all a little more cautious.

The prince and Dami continued their fight, both knowing that to lose would be the end. The prince jumped high using the spear as a pole vault, flying through the air and swinging the point at Dami. Alice looked on as the blade sliced across the rat king's head, severing an ear. Dami howled in pain, slashing out with his tail and smashing the prince to the floor.

Alice screamed and Dami looked towards her, a smile on his face.

"Say goodbye to your little prince." He pulled a blade from his belt.

"This blade has seen so much. I do believe it killed your very own great-grandfather, causing Gabriella to leave and this whole story to begin with, and now full circle it will bring the story to a close."

Laughing, he swung the blade at the prince, its point digging into the prince's side. The prince screamed in pain. Alice collapsed, crying where she stood. This can't be the end! There was still so much to learn so many stories to hear and tales to tell.

Another scream caught her attention. A rat had landed on her gran pinning her to the floor. Her mother swung a branch at the creature, using all her strength to slash it across its face and blind it in one eye. Her Gran stabbed out with her own stick, thrusting it into the rat's side. The rat collapsed with a look of shock on its face, but in doing so, her gran was now trapped under the dying beast.

Others had fallen. They had fought a gallant fight. Many rats lay dead but so did many spiders.

Dami shouted out: "So little prince, this is the end! Have one last look at your precious Alice."

Dami turned and pointed at her with the bloodied blade. He turned back and raised the blade.

"You know you should never have left the safety of your precious kingdom. You should have let us end these albinos to close the chapter on their short, worthless story and no one would have cared."

"I care!" the prince shouted.

Pulling his own knife from his belt he dug it deep into Dami's mouth, as far as he could. He pushed the blade deeper still, slicing the rat's tongue clean from its root.

Dami screamed. Blood pouring from his mouth, he raised his own dagger again, lunging as he collapsed onto the prince.

The rat army roared in anger. Their leader lay prone on top of the prince. Charging at the remaining spiders who were nearly upon them. The sky darkened as dozens and dozens of arrows flew through the air, striking the rats.

Alice looked back to where the arrows had come from, seeing dozens of creatures making their own charge towards the rats. There were spiders, bugs and even a few of the peace-loving grasshoppers. Leading from the front was the king and her brother.

The remaining rat army looked on in shock. Their leader was dead, and hundreds of their fellow rats were lying dead or wounded. The rest decided that the best option was to run, and so they fled, leaving the wounded running for their lives. The spider army gave chase, clearing the battlefield and forming a protective barrier around the spiders.

"Where's my son?" the king shouted, looking for the prince. Alice approached and curtsied.

"There is no need for that, lady Alice. Please where is the prince, where is my son?"

She looked towards the fallen form of Dami and a sadness crossed her face. The king ran forward and heaved at the large brown corpse of Dami. His guards helped pull the prince free.

"Son, please." The king's voice broke at the sight of his son's bloodied and crushed form. "Please son, please don't die." The king cradled the prince and started to cry.

"Dad!" The prince coughed. "Kings don't cry"

The king looked down at the prince. He was bloodied and bruised, but he was alive.

The days passed. The albinos settled into their new homes. Some found their place quickly, learning new skills, helping in the community gardens, or working to help build new homes in this strange new world. Some were understandably scared, being in the bright sunlight out in the open.

The old hermit, well, he found a little plot of land by the kingdom wall, away from the hustle and bustle of the main square but close enough so that others could pop by and enjoy a cup of tea with him.

A few weeks later, when the excitement had all settled down, Alice and her family mourned her father. They remembered his brave and caring ways. The elders gathered to elect a new leader. Normally this would fall to one of them, to a spider with wisdom gained through a life well lived, but these new times had shown that none of them had lived, they had existed and floated through life. None had pushed themselves, and the only one who could be the leader they needed was Alice. At first she refused; she herself was so young and it had only been due to her stubbornness and stupidity to run from her family that they were now part of something bigger.

Her granny and mother both agreed to stand with Alice, to guide her the best they could, and even her little brother admitted he was proud of his big sister.

The sun was out and Alice was showing her brother around. He had soaked up all the wonders of the kingdom, every day wanting to learn more. Today Alice had promised to show him the most amazing sight. Leading him towards the great library, she noticed the look of amazement and wonder in his eyes and it reminded her of the first time she saw the building.

Entering the library, her brother was struck silent, his eyes trying to take it all in.

"This way," Alice said, trying to keep her brother moving.

Past rows and rows of books, Alice explained that this was where the history of the kingdom was written down, including the story of Gabriella, their distant relative.

"There will be plenty of time for this," Alice gestured with her arm. "Time to read, once you have been taught how, to discover our story, and the story of the kingdom. One day all of these stories will be yours. The adventures and places they will take you are beyond anything you could imagine."

"I'm sorry I laughed at you when dad was…" his voice trailed off at the thought of their dad.

"I miss him so much," he continued, with tears in his eyes.

"I know, I miss him too little brother, but that's why we are here." Alice opened the door and led her brother inside the same chamber she had been in, what seemed like a lifetime ago.

"These are the grasshoppers. They are responsible for all of these books. They wish to write down our story. You may not know how to read yet, but you can still tell them everything, all our history and how we came to be here in the kingdom."

She watched as her brother walked off with one of the grasshoppers, happily chatting away. His excitement grew as he shouted details of the albino spiders and their little world, under the floorboards, in that old, long-forgotten bookshop.

Alice walked out of the library, back into the early winter sun. All around her creatures of all sorts were busy harvesting the last of the fruits to see them through the winter, but none were concerned about hunger or going short. They knew that through working together and helping each other they would endure, and no one would take that away.

Making her way to find the prince, Alice smiled for the first time in what seemed like forever. She felt at home and knew there would be so many more adventures to come.

The End

A Fireside Tale

"Come join us, Alice!" Granny waved at her as she walked by a little circle of bugs and critters sitting around a small fire. The wood crackled and spat sparks up into the sky, keeping away the evening chill. The sun had set below the rooftop of the distant bookshop, cloaking the Kingdom in darkness.

Since the Albinos had settled into their new home within the kingdom dozens of moons back, Alice often found herself busy helping settle new arrivals as more and more creatures came looking for a safe place to live.

Alice missed spending time listening to Granny's tales from her youth; adventures within the midnight darkness of the Albinos' world beneath the floorboards of the bookshop. Alice felt some stories were exaggerated for thrills or to keep the little ones in line with the details of monsters in the dark, but either way they were important as they helped remember the past and their history from before they left the darkness.

Seated next to Granny was Kris, one of the apprentice scribes from the Grasshopper clan, ready to record the story so that future generations could enjoy it for themselves in the magnificent library. One of the grasshoppers would always join in these little tellings, and quite often two or three would be in attendance not to write the story down but just because they enjoyed the stories as much as the children.

Settling in a gap between a ladybird whom Alice didn't recognise was another new arrival from out in the wastelands, and a wolf spider named Mel.

Mel and her brother George had become close friends, and were normally out getting into some sort of mischief. It was nice to see her brother able to live a normal life.

"So, you have all heard the story of Gabriella and the great escape to the old bookshop by lady Alice's distant relatives!" Alice's Granny stopped for dramatic effect.

"Between those early days and the return to the kingdom, it wasn't all just hiding in the dark and forgetting the past. As a young girl, I was very much like lady Alice, looking for more, trying to make sense of it all, as if the very spirit of Gabriella was calling to me."

Looking off into the distance, Granny's eyes seemed to glaze over. Her face was deep in concentration, the soft white fur across her brow wrinkled and lined.

"Where was I...ahh yes, the spirit of Gabriella. When I was about the same age as Mel here..."

Mel smiled at being mentioned. Alice had also learnt that in many of the stories her Granny told, she would make them relevant to the audience. Whether mentioning the age of an audience member, or including someone with a similar name, this kept the listening youngsters keen, wanting to know more as they bought into the story.

"It was around the time of the Hunter's Moon, at the end of the month mankind had called October, when ghosts and demons walked the Earth. My friends and I had gone to the hermit's house at the edge of town. At the time it stood empty, after the previous occupant had passed away a long time before. The building, smaller than most in the town, stood alone. Its garden was overgrown, and the walls were covered in midnight brambles, the short, spiked creepers that grew in the darkness below the floorboards." Granny stopped again, making sure everyone was listening.

Alice had often gone searching for the berries that the brambles produced. Walking with her grandmother, they would normally find just enough to feed her family for a few days. Her father particularly enjoyed the under ripe ones with a bitter taste. She smiled at the memory of her father whom she still missed dearly after the rats attacked their home trying to end the Albinos once and for all.

"So there we are, standing outside the little house, daring each other to go in," Granny continued.

"Go on Dorothy," said Joe, who would, in the future, become the very hermit who lived in the house during Alice's adventure. He now lived on the outskirts of the kingdom in peace and solitude.

Dot hated it when Joe called her Dorothy. Only her mum and dad did that, especially when she had caused a little too much mischief around the town.

"You go!" Dot egged Joe on herself.

Standing by were the other three of this little group. There was Samantha — well, Sam to her friends; she was Joe's twin sister, younger by three minutes as Joe often reminded them. Florence, the oldest of the group and normally the one to come up with these crazy ideas (but she somehow never seemed to go first); and Freddie, a brave and energetic albino, who would more often than not lead the way on these adventures.

"Out the way!" Freddie pushed past the group towards the threatening door, with the surrounding brambles creating a ring of teeth hundreds deep.

Dot looked on as Freddie approached. She watched as he flexed his muscles and started to pull at the brambles.

"What are you staring at?" Flo teased.

Dot and Flo had both discussed Freddie's young, muscular form and Flo would tease her friend about it.

Dot blushed and made an exaggerated effort to change the subject.

Freddie turned and smiled. He knew Dot liked him, and he felt the same, but they were still young, and he enjoyed the friendship he had, not just with Dot but with the whole group.

With the doorway clear, the group stood staring at the foreboding space beyond.

"So go on!" Joe shouted from the back.

It was Dot's turn to push forward, so she stepped towards the door, telling herself there was nothing to be scared of; there were no monsters here, just imagination and tall tales.

The floor was immaculate, which was strange. Even here in the darkness of their little world, dust would settle and cover anything that stayed still. But there wasn't a single speck.

Taking another slow step forward, Dot pushed the thought to the back of her head.

"Rahhhhhhhhh!" Joe shouted at the top of his voice. Sam and Flo screamed. Freddie slipped on the spotless floor, and ran for the door and the open space outside. But he crashed into the little table, knocking the few trinkets on its spotless surface over, sending them crashing to the floor below.

Dot turned, laughing at her friends. Joe stood, disappointed that he was unable to frighten her.

"Pick that stuff up." Dot pointed at the bits and bobs laying scattered on the floor.

"Who cares, no one lives here," Joe replied

Again, Dot couldn't put her finger on it. The place didn't seem to be abandoned.

"That's not the point, we leave it as we find it," she replied with a sternness in her voice that she would often find herself using later in life with her grandchildren Alice and George.

Freddie and Joe headed off towards the rear of the house, giggling as they whispered to each other.

Although Dot fancied Freddie, he sometimes annoyed her with his childish ways. She prepared herself for them to play another joke, jumping out at them or some other such trick.

"Hey look at this!" Flo was standing next to the cold hearth but what was strange was the silken covering, not unlike a spider's web, but thicker and matted together.

"What do you think it's from? The rest of the house is spotless," Flo said, as she gently lifted a piece of the strange substance from the floor.

"You spotted that as well" Dot replied, looking around. "I'm not sure, but I hope whatever made it is long gone."

The scream made them both jump and rush in from the living room towards the back of the house.

"Guys, where are you?"

Another scream, blood-curdling, primal. Something was frightened.

As Granny Dot described the scene, sitting there around the fire with the others listening intently, she screamed at the top of her voice.

Mel and the others, even Alice, all jumped.

"Hahaha!" Dorothy sat laughing at her little joke.

"Granny, that wasn't funny" Alice tried to sound serious but couldn't help smiling.

"Oh come now child, what's a little scare. Now where was I? Oh, yes. So, rushing towards the sound of the scream, we ran to find our friends."

There on the floor laid Freddie, out cold but no obvious injuries. It looked like he had fainted.

"Where's Joe and Sam?" Florence looked worried at the sight of their friend laying on the floor. Dot was leaning over him, gently coaxing him to consciousness.

A crash drew their attention towards the hall, as a shadow shot past the kitchen doorway.

"What was that?"

Florence stepped back, just a little, but enough that she was now behind Dot.

"It must be one of the others. There's no one else here, there hasn't been for years."

"Sam... Joe, is that you?"

The noise seemed to come from all around them; a clicking like someone tapping a nail against the floor.

Click Click from the left.

Click Click Now the right, what was happening?

"Who's there!" Dot shouted, trying to sound braver than she felt. "Hello?"

Click... Click... Click.

The shadow edged around the door frame, and slowly came further and further into the room, and as the light from the moon moss outside the window caught the shadow a purple shimmer fluttered across it.

"Hello?" Dot stepped forward, showing her front legs to be empty,

"Hello, we mean you no harm."

Click... Click

The shadow stopped.

With a sudden flash, it grew in size, unfolding its wings. Dot had never seen anything so beautiful. In the middle, a fur-covered body with a dozen spindly legs, a small head with huge shimmering multicoloured eyes, the wings were outstanding, covered in patterns like nothing she had ever seen.

"What is it" Florence managed to stutter.

"I think it's a moth. I haven't seen one before, but have heard stories of them."

Click Click

"I don't think it's dangerous, I think we just startled it."

Sam and Joe appeared at the other end of the kitchen. The moth turned and flapped its wings, causing a draft across the room.

Sam hid behind her brother, letting out a scream.

"Shhh!" Dot said turning to her friends. "It's harmless."

Sam held her mouth, muffling her scream.

Dorothy stepped closer still, reaching for the moth, trying to calm the creature and stop the hurricane-like winds it was creating.

"Please, calm down, we didn't mean to scare you! What is your name?"

Click click "My name... Is Chanzel."

The sound was hard to understand, like each syllable was pronounced with their tongue stuck to the roof of their mouth.

"My name is Dorothy... Dot, I'm pleased to meet you, these are my friends Sam and her brother Joe, Florence and the one on the floor is Freddie."

"Why is he asleep?" Chanzel stepped towards the prone form of the albino spider on the floor.

"He...he was shocked, that is all"

"I'm sorry, did I do that?"

Freddie started to stir, "What... happened?"

He saw the moth standing there over him, "Aghhhhh!"

The moth jumped back, flapping its wings and sending another gust around the room.

"Stop, Freddie! This is Chanzel, she means no harm."

Slowly the young spider calmed down and stood next to his friends. "Where did it come from?"

"I don't know," it answered.

"It talks."

"It seems to have some knowledge of our language, yes." Turning to the moth, "How long have you been here?"

"I remember crawling into the darkness as a caterpillar, my parents had gone, my siblings had all left the nest, and I was alone."

The moth looked sad as it tried to think of the words to continue its story.

"After waiting for what seemed like a lifetime, I found my way here. It was dry and warmer than out in the world."

"Sorry, you came from outside? There is nothing out there, just death and monsters."

"Yes, it's hard out there, but there is life."

"So what do you plan to do? This is no place for a winged beast, there is no space to fly."

"I was getting ready to leave. After awaking from my chrysalis, I need to find my family."

"You can stay as long as you want, and leave when ready. No one lives in this house any more, and you are more than welcome to stay."

"Thank you, that's so kind, but once my wings are fully dried, I shall be going."

Dorothy looked around at the group who sat with her. Every word was like magic to their ears.

"What happened next?" they all shouted, eager to hear the end of the story before they were called home to their beds.

"Well, Chanzel left, we escorted her to the edge of town, but at the time none of us were brave enough to go any further than that. We all promised to keep our encounter secret. No one would ever believe us anyway. We would only talk about Chanzel when we were alone at the old house."

Suddenly, from above a shadow fell across the group, letting out a loud clicking noise. The youngsters screamed as the winged beast flapped above them and a small tornado formed, nearly extinguishing the fire. The dust flew, and the creature continued to flap its huge colourful wings, the flames glittering across its beautiful fur.

Dorothy laughed, her wicked sense of humour making her smile.

"Everyone, I would like you to meet Chaz. Great-great-granddaughter of Chanzel!"

"A pleasure to meet you all!" the moth folded its beautiful iridescent wings, its eyes reflecting the moonlight from above.

As the other youngsters said their goodbyes, Alice stood talking to the Chaz. She had seen many winged creatures within the kingdom, each with its own magical patten of colours across their wings and body.

"I don't think we have met before. Do you live outside the kingdom?"

"Yes, she does." Dorothy walked over, having seen the youngsters on their way. "The kingdom isn't the only place where creatures all live together. If you head past the bookshop and keep going, you will come to a place that man once called a park, no more than wasteland with small bushes as far as you can see.

All except one singular tree, a mighty oak, home to dozens of winged species."

"It sounds amazing, I didn't know that other places existed."

"That's why I am here!" Chaz spoke in her tight-clipped voice. "We would like to invite you and your prince to a gathering. There is to be a carnation, I am to become queen, and it is time that the Kingdom and Oakland joined together!"

Alice smiled at the thought. It was time for another adventure.

ACKNOWLEDGEMENTS

Thank you to everyone who supported me in the writing and production of the word spider.

My beta readers Hayley and Anna.

My kids for their honest views (apparently spiders are scary).

Debbie, www.Debbieburkeauthor.com for her editing skills and unending advice and help and guidance.

Jon, www.Jonstubbington.com for bringing my vision to life with his amazing art work.

Without all of the above, "The Word Spider" would never have been published.

CHRIS HORN has worked within the rail industry for sixteen years. Having had an interest in reading and a very active imagination for many years, in 2019 he entered a short story contest and "The Word Spider" was born. Telling stories either made up or reading some well-known children's books to his own kids, Chris finds they are a way to escape the ordinary day-to-day and transport the listener to a different world. Like the main character Alice, from "The Word Spider," Chris also enjoys seeing new places and going on adventures.

With book two in production and an anthology of Granny's adventures, Chris hopes the world of "The Word Spider" will entertain for years to come.

Printed in Great Britain
by Amazon

75752754R10058